P9-BBN-448

The
Three R's

by Belinda Dancing Bear
illustrated by Cheryl Kirk Noll

HOUGHTON MIFFLIN HARCOURT
School Publishers

Copyright © by Houghton Mifflin Harcourt Publishing Company

All rights reserved. No part of this work may be reproduced or transmitted in any form or by any means, electronic or mechanical, including photocopying or recording, or by any information storage and retrieval system, without the prior written permission of the copyright owner unless such copying is expressly permitted by federal copyright law. Requests for permission to make copies of any part of the work should be addressed to Houghton Mifflin Harcourt School Publishers, Attn: Permissions, 6277 Sea Harbor Drive, Orlando, Florida 32887-6777.

Printed in China

ISBN-13: 978-0-547-01668-9
ISBN-10: 0-547-01668-9

12 13 14 15 0940 19 18 17 16
4500569761

If you have received these materials as examination copies free of charge, Houghton Mifflin Harcourt School Publishers retains title to the materials and they may not be resold. Resale of examination copies is strictly prohibited.

Possession of this publication in print format does not entitle users to convert this publication, or any portion of it, into electronic format.

Carmen, Marcus, Lee, and Toni always sat together. This time, though, they were teamed up for a project in Mrs. Kennedy's class. The four of them were supposed to be working. It wasn't really happening.

"Come on, show me some of those photos," Carmen said, as she elbowed Marcus.

"You'll see them soon enough," he replied, turning his digital camera away from her.

"How long until the end of class?" Lee asked.

Toni glared at her friends. "Look," she said. "So far, we've met twice. We haven't even developed an idea for our community service project. The other groups are already deciding who will do what on their projects. If we don't come up with an idea today, Mrs. Kennedy will chew us out."

"Stay cool, Toni," Carmen grumbled.

Toni pulled out the project guidelines Mrs. Kennedy had passed out a few days ago. They would help the groups get organized, she had explained. "Step 1—*Brainstorm Ideas*," Toni read aloud. "Well?" she said, feeling a little anxious since the group was already falling behind. She looked at the other three members of the group expectantly. "Got any ideas?"

Marcus was still scrolling through photos on his digital camera. Carmen was creating an elaborate doodle on an otherwise blank sheet of notebook paper. Lee was making notes for a new episode of *Manta Ray*, a comic strip he'd invented about a heroic race of fish who patrol Earth's criminal seas in the year 5000, after humans have destroyed all life on land.

According to Lee's comic, 3,000 years from now, humans abandon Earth, leaving behind toxic substances that spill into the oceans and affect the mental state of sea creatures. Most of them turn into lawless hoodlums—except for the manta rays, which try their best to keep order.

"So, any ideas?" Toni repeated.

Carmen glanced up from her work. "Sorry. What did you say?" The two boys ignored her completely.

Toni sighed. She realized that the community service project was the last thing on their minds. *Why did Mrs. K assign me to this group?* she wondered. *Probably because she knows that we're all friends. But does Mrs. K have any idea how hard it is to get serious with these guys?*

Toni scanned the classroom, looking for something that might inspire a project idea. The words *REDUCE, REUSE,* and *RECYCLE* had been written on the bulletin board since September. A trash can overflowing with paper stood on the floor below the word *REDUCE,* while an empty blue recycling bin sat forlornly below the word *RECYCLE.*

"Hey, how about a project on recycling?" Toni suggested.

"Boring," Marcus said.

"Reject, relocate, refrigerate," Carmen offered.

"I know some *people* I'd like to recycle," Lee added.

"You guys are just hopeless," Toni said, barely able to hide her annoyance.

"You got *that* right," Marcus replied. Carmen giggled.

Then the bell rang and Mrs. Kennedy made an announcement. "I trust that each group has made good progress on its community service project." Mrs. K wasn't checking on the groups very carefully since she expected them to complete their projects independently. "It's good preparation for middle school," she explained. She continued, "Tomorrow you should begin Step 3—*Gather Information.* Any questions?"

Toni glumly shoved her books into her backpack. What on earth was she going to do? She wanted to do well on the project, but her friends were making it impossible. Not wanting them to see her frustration, Toni quickly slipped out of the classroom.

On the way to the bus stop, Carmen, Lee, and Marcus caught up with her. "Hey, Toni, don't be mad," Marcus said. "It's just one little project. We'll get it done."

Then Carmen spoke up. "He's right, Toni. Don't sweat it."

Lee chimed in, "Hey, Toni—Marcus and Carmen are coming over to my house. Mama made pizza last night, and there's lots left over. Wanna come?"

Toni shrugged. "Maybe."

Toni gazed out the window as the bus rumbled down Third Street toward Lee's house. Old snow from last week's storm, black with soot, formed massive piles along the sidewalks. The sooty snow matched Toni's mood.

Sometimes Toni didn't understand her friends. But in many ways, she and they were alike. They all lived on the same block. They had attended Grover Cleveland Elementary School together since first grade. Their parents worked hard, although the money never seemed to stretch far enough. Clothes, toys, and bikes were passed from one brother or sister to the next. That was life for most of the kids in their neighborhood.

Toni didn't really mind. Her mom did as much as she could for Toni and her sisters. She worked two jobs and often wasn't home until after 9:00 p.m. Still, she always managed to make important occasions such as birthdays into special events.

Toni respected her mom for working so hard to take care of the family. She never had the chance to complete her own education, but Toni had big plans for *her* future. She would go to college, on scholarships if necessary.

Toni's pals didn't seem to think much about their futures. According to Mr. Peña, their art teacher, Carmen had the natural talent to be a first-rate illustrator. But Carmen didn't have much confidence in her abilities. Toni could tell that art school wasn't even on Carmen's radar screen. Lately, it seemed like elementary school wasn't on her radar screen, either.

Marcus's photographs showed that he, too, had talent. But like Carmen, Marcus didn't think he was exceptional in any way. He just shrugged when anyone asked him what he wanted to be; when it came to school, he coasted, doing as little in his classes as he could get by with.

And Lee? Lee had the best imagination of anyone Toni had ever met. His science fiction stories were practically legendary, and he read stuff that would fry an eighth grader's brain. If anyone was capable of doing super well in school, it was Lee, but he acted like school was too much trouble.

It's weird, Toni thought. *Outside school, we have a great time together. It's only* in *school that our differences show up.*

As the bus screeched to a halt, the friends tumbled out the back door and walked briskly down Third Street toward Lee's. As they reached the corner of Third and Palou, Carmen yelled out, "Look!" A rusty little blue tricycle had been set on the corner, next to a trash can filled with other old stuff. "My little brother could totally use that," she said, examining the find more closely. "All it needs is a little paint and a new rear wheel." She picked up the tricycle and flashed a giant smile. "Hey, Marcus, take a picture!"

Marcus pulled off his gloves, fished for his camera, and snapped a photo. "This is the *before* picture," he announced with a gleam in his eye. "After you fix it up, I'll take an *after* picture."

While sitting around talking and eating tasty pizza, Toni's mind wandered. She envied Marcus's creative ways. Some people keep diaries or journals, but Marcus didn't particularly like writing. So he took photos as a sort of visual journal. He'd probably already set some kind of record for taking more pictures than any other kid his age. Marcus had also created his own blog. He posted photos on it so his friends would know what he was up to. Toni figured that the *before* and *after* tricycle pictures would eventually end up there, too.

The next day, on the bus ride to school, Carmen pointed out to Lee an old green barbecue that someone had abandoned on the corner of Third and Maxwell. "Wow! My dad sure could use that. Our old one is messed up—the coals burned through the bottom. If that barbecue's still there on the way home, I'm gonna rescue it and clean it up. Thanks, Carmen."

"Anytime I can help," Carmen replied.

It was Lee's lucky day. The group spotted the barbecue on the way home and got off the bus to retrieve it. Marcus pulled out his camera and snapped a *before* shot. "Let's see how well you clean up this old thing," he teased.

By the end of the week, little had changed at school. Toni's group had not made any progress, and now she was really getting worried. Time was running out, and she wasn't sure what to do.

In the meantime, Lee's *Manta Ray* project had made big progress. Over the last few days, he had created several gripping stories based on the hero rays, but his illustrations weren't that good—and he knew it. So, he had proposed an idea to Carmen. "What do you think about doing the art for *Manta Ray?*" he'd asked. "I plan to sell a million copies. That means you'll get rich, too."

"I'll do *one*," she had agreed, a bit reluctantly. "We'll see about the rest." Carmen had worked hard on the first illustration before passing it on to Lee.

During sixth period on Friday, when they should have been working on their group project, Marcus asked, "What's up with *Manta Ray?*" Lee gladly explained that the rays had slain most of the barracudas, but a few exceptionally vicious fish had escaped. Now they were hiding in the deepest part of the ocean, in a dark, creepy gorge known as the Mariana Trench. To catch these villains, the manta rays needed the help of the incredibly ugly, but powerful, eyeless slugs.

Then Lee paused as he thumbed through a messy pile of papers. "And now I finally have a piece of great art for my first comic strip!" he continued, proudly waving Carmen's illustration in his friends' faces.

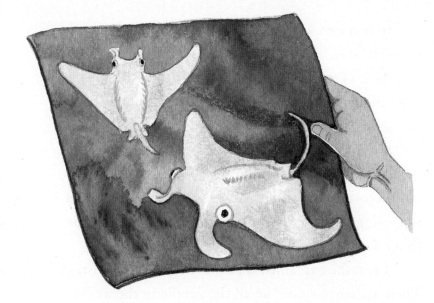

Marcus, setting down his camera, gazed spellbound at a beautiful picture of two manta rays. They were swimming gracefully in an inky blue sea. "Wow! That is awesome! Can I take a picture of it?" he asked.

"Ask Carmen," Lee replied.

"A picture of a picture? Suit yourself," Carmen muttered. She shrugged like she didn't care one way or the other. But Toni knew Carmen well enough to see that she was deeply flattered by the praise.

That night, the first illustration for *Manta Ray* appeared on Marcus's blog. He had also posted some *before* and *after* photos— two of Carmen's tricycle and two of Lee's green barbecue. He titled these *TOSSED AND FOUND*. Marcus wasn't sure what to title the picture of the manta rays. He finally decided on *HERO FISH FIGHT UNDERSEA CRIME*.

In just two weeks, the community service project would be due, and Toni's group had not even decided what to do yet. *It's time I make a decision for the group,* Toni thought. *There's no time left to keep trying to motivate these guys.*

So Toni went back to her original idea and told her friends her plan. "Listen. We're going to have to do our project on recycling. We can call it 'Reawaken to Recycling.' I know the title is lame, but if we get this thing done, we can probably get a decent grade."

Then she explained that they could make posters. Their audience would be all the people in the world who walk by recycling bins but throw recyclables into the regular trash anyway.

By this time, Lee was back to his own writing, Marcus was fiddling with his camera, and Carmen was working on another colorful drawing of the undersea world. She had decided that she liked drawing pictures for *Manta Ray.* *At least we* look *like we're working on something serious,* Toni thought.

"So, I really need your help," she announced, finally getting their full attention. "Lee, can you write a catchy slogan?" He agreed. Then Marcus, feeling like he should contribute just a little, said he would photograph an empty recycling bin next to a trash can filled with recyclable stuff. Carmen said she would draw some illustrations.

On the bus ride home that day, the friends noticed a dumpster outside an empty storefront. The dumpster bulged with leftover inventory from a stationery supply store that had gone out of business. They could see a whole box full of notebooks lying at the top of the pile. Plus, pads of drawing paper, rolls of canvas, and display racks for greeting cards jutted out of the overflowing mass of materials. The supplies weren't in perfect shape, but they were certainly usable.

"Look at all that stuff!" Carmen exclaimed. "I sure could use some of those drawing pads, but there's so much other stuff. Marcus, take some pictures of that bin!" Carmen instructed.

"Maybe you can post them on the Internet," she suggested. "I bet a lot of people would come and get this stuff, if they knew it was here. I'm going to come back early tomorrow morning for sure!"

That night, Marcus uploaded his photos of the discarded art supplies and the street address of the storefront on a Web site he knew about. The site's slogan was *JUNK FOR ONE—TREASURE FOR ANOTHER*. Anyone who had no more use for an object posted a description of it and his or her contact information. Then anyone who wanted that object contacted the person and arranged to pick it up—for free.

Word about the art supplies spread. By the end of the weekend, people—including Carmen—had claimed the paper, canvas, and display racks. On Monday, as the friends rode to school, it appeared that everything usable had been collected. As a result, the dumpster was almost empty.

As if hypnotized, Carmen gazed at the bin until it was out of sight. Then she said quietly, "I've got it."

"Got what?" Lee asked.

"I've got a great idea for the community service project. I know what we should do."

The others gave her their full attention, curious about how a dumpster could have triggered such an idea. "Listen," Carmen began. "People are always unloading old stuff they don't want anymore, like the tricycle and the barbecue—and those things were still usable. They just needed some fixing up. And the art supplies... some of that stuff like paper is really expensive. So, even though it wasn't perfect, it was fine for drawing. If we hadn't rescued all those things, they'd all have ended up as landfill somewhere. Right?"

"Right," Toni said eagerly. "So what's your idea?"

"We can start a new Web site. It can feature pictures and descriptions of abandoned but usable stuff people see around, like the tricycle. Then anyone who needs something can go and get it. People can add to the site from all over the city!"

Lee exclaimed, "It's brilliant!" Everyone agreed. They could launch the site during the project presentation.

"Hey—a manta ray can be our mascot," Toni suggested. "It can be like a voice from the future warning people not to clutter the earth with discarded junk—or else!"

For once, the group couldn't wait for sixth period. They knew they had some serious catching up to do, but when they sat down at the table together, they didn't quite know where to begin. After Toni pulled out the project guidelines, the team suddenly realized they had already completed Steps 1 and 3 of their new project. But they still had to do Step 2—*Assign Roles.* That seemed like a good place to start.

"Okay," Toni said with authority. "Marcus, you can create the site since you're the technology expert. Lee, you can write the text for the site." Then Carmen, excited, volunteered to design the logo.

"Carmen and Lee, you guys should also decide which manta ray to use as our mascot—assuming you want the illustration to appear," Toni added. Finally, Toni said she'd write up a description of the project.

The week seemed to fly by. The more the friends worked on their project, the more certain they were of its absolute brilliance. By Friday, they were finished.

On the day of the project presentations, Marcus hooked up his computer to a projector so that the class could see what was on his computer screen. When the group's turn to present came, Carmen explained the project and how they had come up with the idea. She pointed out that in the process of rescuing junk, they had stumbled on their project idea and completed some of it without even knowing it. Then Toni flipped off the lights, and Marcus displayed the site's entry screen.

Now, it was Lee's turn to speak. He explained why the group chose a manta ray as its mascot and introduced his *Manta Ray* comics. "I created the comic just for fun," he began. "But then I realized I could use the manta ray to warn humans to change their wasteful ways. By the way, Carmen created these awesome illustrations."

Next, Marcus spoke. "I'll show you how our site works," he said, advancing to the next screen.

"This screen describes some reusable things that we found on the street and shows their locations on a city map," Marcus explained. "I scanned a map and uploaded it to the site. When you want to post an item you've seen, you click on the location on the map where you saw the item. The manta ray icon—which Carmen drew—pops into place on the map, along with a number. Then you write a description of your item. Anyone who wants it goes and gets it. I think the map is the site's most useful feature," he commented.

Maxwell Street

Third Street

Palou Street

1 Small blue tricycle—needs some paint and a new rear wheel. Corner of Third Street and Palou

2 Green barbecue on wheels—good condition, needs a scrub. Corner of Third Street and Maxwell

Last of all, Toni explained how the site would help the community. "Not only will it help remove discarded items from city streets—it will also reduce landfill. It will encourage people to reuse things instead of throwing them away. And, it will help people save money." When she was finished, all four members of the group stood together and recited the site's motto:

The Three R's:
Reclaim! Repair! Reuse!
It's the Manta Way!

Toni flipped on the lights and looked around. The looks
of total admiration on her classmates' faces were obvious.
Mrs. Kennedy beamed with pride. "I knew that this creative
team was cooking up something absolutely brilliant," she said.
"Outstanding job!"

Toni looked at her three friends. They were each standing
tall. They were smiling the unmistakable smiles of people who
knew that they had done something exceptional.

Responding

✔️ **TARGET SKILL** **Author's Purpose** What is Belinda Dancing Bear's purpose in writing *The Three R's*? Copy and complete the chart below. Add the author's purpose as well as details from the story that support it.

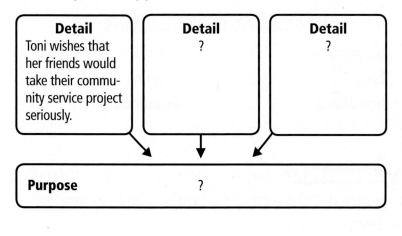

Detail	**Detail**	**Detail**
Toni wishes that her friends would take their community service project seriously.	?	?

Purpose ?

Write About It

Text to Self Think about a community service project you have participated in. Write a letter to a friend, telling about the project and your role in it.

✔ TARGET VOCABULARY

assuming	launch
developed	mental
episodes	record
feature	thumbed
incredibly	villains

EXPAND YOUR VOCABULARY

barracudas	landfill
blog	slogan
hoodlums	uploaded

✔ **TARGET SKILL** **Author's Purpose** Use text details to figure out the author's viewpoint and reasons for writing.

✔ **TARGET STRATEGY** **Monitor/Clarify** As you read, notice what isn't making sense. Find ways to figure out the parts that are confusing.

GENRE **Realistic Fiction** is a present-day story with events that could take place in real life.